SELLIER

CONFESSIONS OF AN ALIEN
MAROONED ON EARTH III

1

Other books by Van Heyden

On Conquering Things

Poetry My Mother Would've Approved
Poetry My Mother Would Not Have Approved
Poetry Even Your Mother Would Approve

What Kids Know That Adults Have Forgot

Confessions of an Alien Marooned on Earth I

FOX AND FALCON -
Confessions of an Alien Marooned on Earth II

The Reincarnation of Edgar Allan Poe

Essays From A Dead Poet

VELVET GLOVES PUBLISHING
© 2013, 2020
All RIGHTS RESERVED
www.velvetglovespub.com

SELLIER

C. Van Heyden

SELLIER

Contents

C. Van Heyden

RECAP

Sellier is a planet that doesn't forget. It's inhabitants remember perfectly their past and their past lives. So, when Elvis returns finally, he is right where he wants to be to vindicate himself, while revealing the evil things he did that he was not caught for and punished.

And while he's actively setting the score straight, he meets a woman who is strangely very much like Catherine, only Catherine isn't on Sellier. She is back on Earth!

When Elvis Apolliani finally met with success in Peru, with the help of Mrs. Amparo, hooking up with the flying saucer aliens he had decided he would not press Catherine nor myself to go with him, back to his home planet. He rightly new that if we, Catherine and I, didn't fit in there was no way really for us to return to Earth. So, Elvis met the alien spacecraft flyers, and with the help of and her ability to harvest thought from them, got them to agree to take Elvis to Sellier. But in return they wanted something that they perceived he might have, when he told them of the transshipment area he had invaded to find a way back. It was the token that Bharabas (BHAR-AH-BAS) had left him as a memento as much as a talisman. The token that symbolized the technology of teleportation, a technology the fly boys, from who knows where, didn't have.

This he related to me, Joshua, in a letter quickly jotted on a piece of stiff cardboard that was handy.

Later, and I still don't know how, Elvis was in touch with me, I would call it one-way *long distance telepathy*. Naturally he told me to convey this also to Catherine. Here is what he told me.

SELLIER

TAKE OFF

C. Van Heyden

I boarded the space craft (saucer like) with the indispensable help of Serena (Mrs. Amparo), who did a bang-up job of interpreting the alien speech / telepathy to me and mine to them. The child-like* aliens were jazzed about the token I showed them and on that alone decided they could trust me. Since I had no suit, and wasn't built like them, which was as far as I could perceive a rubbery plastic type body, they put me in a coffin type apparatus which was pressurized and even had oxygen which they needed very little of themselves. I was relieved to find out that they didn't have to freeze me, just protect me from the pressure changes. I have to admit when these flyboys first landed I was *very* apprehensive as to the outcome since they being from, jeez, another part of the universe they couldn't possibly have any respect for other planetary life forms, you know how invaders and explorers usually are? As far as I could tell the ship wasn't armed with any weapons, but then nobody was firing on them or attempting to drag them off somewhere for interrogation. Something, although, told me that if I crossed them or attempted any more than being just a passenger they would make

---

* They *looked* child-like but that was only because, I believe, their size was hand selected due to the confines of their spaceship-not a lot of room.

me regret it. I wasn't one of them and never would be.

Now, here's the real great part: when I showed them the star map that Lexington prepared for me for them, they showed more interest and they told Mrs. Amparo they knew where this place (Sellier) was. Man that was the best news ever! I almost got the feeling that they liked me. That was the other piece of news which convinced me that I would trust them and go with them. But when I asked them how long? *to get there* the interpretation came back garbled even to Serena, but I didn't care. I was going no matter what.

When Serena and I had hugged I handed her my letter to Catherine and said goodbye. I was escorted onto the ship and immediately we took off. I felt a little vulnerable. Once in the pressurized unit I could hear nothing and see only the dark grey ceiling above me. The only reason I asked how long? was that even though these saucers were known to dart around fantastically fast, I still believed that stars were so far as to make journeys between them very long, and I would get very hungry if I didn't eat. Even this Serena was able to fathom to the aliens, although I get that they probably, since they had visited Earth many times before, knew already I had an animal type body that needed nourishment regularly.

In a matter of minutes I was hooked up to what on Earth would be called an intravenous, only this one went directly to the stomach and was very pleasant. Amazingly. I even got the sensation of muscle movement from some external source, so I concluded that I was not the first human or animal body they had transported.

We were en route.

C. Van Heyden

SELLIER

ARRIVAL

C. Van Heyden

J osh, we've arrived! This is so SO incredible. I recall this place like it was only yesterday. Beautiful too. Let me explain. On Earth there was once a civilization called Atlantis, a very *very* advanced type civilization. Well this planet Sellier, at least where the aliens dropped me is a whole lot like the mythical Atlantis, don't ask me how I know. Populations back on Earth would be astounded to see what I am seeing, and to know that they are not alone, not even close. You know, because I took you through some of your bad times here, remember? But for every bad time there are many many good times. After all that commotion, revolution, purging, violence and murder I am looking at...well god if only you could see what I am seeing. Perhaps I can send an image as well as my word thoughts. (But he couldn't, so he described Sellier to me.) First of all the daylight is very much like Earth, and the air, yes air. I wasn't so sure that would be what I found, is practically the same, but definitely sweeter and purer. And the land, at least where I am looking, is all beautifully terraced and verdant and lush and there's so much of it. I haven't seen any water, but I'll bet there's oceans or enormous lakes.

There are some peculiar towers placed around in a circle but very pretty, like tall pagodas. And there are roads, and trees with very smooth and very hard bark. There's even flowers! This is just too amazing. Some object just flew overhead at phenomenal speed and disappeared over a low mountain. Guess they have airships. I don't remember them, but I was sent off in something like a rocket when I was exiled. Those aliens were very smart to drop me away from any *seeing eyes.* It may be that if I parachuted in, this is funny, I would wind up a specimen on my own true planet. I'm going to stop transmitting for awhile until I locate and figure out a good way to introduce the fact to the citizens that I've returned. Note: How Elvis knew when to reach me in waking hours, I can not right now explain.

Several hours passed: I'm looking at Greco-Romanesque type building and now I know that I AM home. This is what I remember so well. There are people thronging this modest city shall I call it, don't know, have nothing to compare it to. But I have met one inhabitant so far who stopped to converse with me, and I could tell from their expression they knew I was from not their area. He or she, can't tell quite yet, everyone looks so healthy and vital, all wearing loose fitting clothing of some thin lightweight material. Oh, I forgot to mention the temperature is mild, get that. It is so natural like back in Peru I didn't even realize it, unlike the times I stepped off planes in China and found the heat unbearable. I'm still wearing my jumpsuit which is getting some pretty strange looks from time to time. Must be the wrinkles from lying "in state" for so long ha-ha. Never did find out how long the trip from Earth to Sellier was. I don't know what they eat, should say what *we* eat, now that I'm stranded back on my planet. Judging from the general body types I would say food like back on Earth, but I have a sneaking suspicion it leans toward fruits and vegetables; there's no one so far that has an ounce of fat on them.

And then Elvis quit transmitting for awhile.

C. Van Heyden

SELLIER

CATHERINE

C. Van Heyden

Back on Earth, Catherine was struck dumb when she read Elvis's letter. She told me that she had no idea. Catherine in her naïveté believed everything, all the white lies, Elvis told her, but I assured her he was not lying about having loved her for the time they were together. This I was sure of as Elvis had confided this fact to me more than once.

When she read the part of how Elvis had wanted her to come along with him, but he was very hesitant knowing it would be a one-way, she cried. She told me, "I would have gone, I trusted him. Wherever he wanted to go I would've have gone, even to another planet." Then she got angry. "Damn it Joshua. He didn't even give me the choice." I could say nothing to console her. I too, felt left out. And now that he had succeeded, I even wished to hell he had invited me, even though I committed to be Master Dick's beneficiary and estate holder. I at least had some knowledge of his planet, in fact Sellier was once my home also.

Catherine thought of telling her father Frank that she had been abandoned but rescinded the idea. I was able with Master Dick's financial help to make a voyage back to the U.S. to be with Catherine, as it was Elvis' last desire and instruction. In any other situation I would have done much the same as brothers do for each other when one goes off to war and dies, and the other takes on the responsibilities for the widowed wife, even though Catherine was not a widow technically. We spent many times together until I could stay no longer and returned to Fengcheng and my place supporting Master Dick. It was a few weeks after I arrived back in *my new home* that Elvis started broadcasting, so that may tell readers how long it took between planets. Master Dick was so pleased to hear of the success of Elvis' daring attempt. He said nothing more on the subject ever again.

SELLIER

REGALLIA

C. Van Heyden

When next I received messages from Elvis he had met and *spoken* with an inhabitant of Sellier and this is what he told me.

Josh, you won't believe it, but I've met a girl...a female, a woman, she's gorgeous and so intelligent and she's a lot like Catherine in many ways! (Boy, was Elvis excited) The women here all wear their hair short, like the page boy look but much prettier. Her name is Regallia. She is of marriageable age, she told me right out. Apparently sex is not so hidden and manipulated on Sellier. She's a very bold person in her occupation. Seems she is an engineer by trade, but one who is hired by companies to seek out rich deposits of minerals, especially uranium. Well paid, and when I told her who I was SHE REMEMBERD ME! SHE REMEMBERD MY BEING EXILED. SHE REMEMBERED HER LIFE AT THE TIME OF THE UPHEAVAL AND DEPOSING OF THE ALMIGHTY AND THE CONSEQUENT DEMISE OF THAT WORLD. (At this point I thought my head was coming off so rambunctious were his thoughts coming through very strongly and he continued:) MY FRIENDS ARE STILL HERE! MY FRIENDS ARE STILL HERE!! (Then nothing) I thought he was going to drop unconscious from the exertion. Then very slowly and very carefully he explained that on Sellier the inhabitants don't FORGET. They remember everything. That makes for a very safe and sane civilization. People don't do stupid or bad things ordinarily. They know that they will live again, and so no one can control them with fear or threats. (I hadn't thought of that.)

Elvis told me that they communicate with thought also, and he didn't *have to* learn Sellier's spoken languages because there were none, but they did have some, for signs and written materials. That's why he could read Stockton's thoughts and even my thoughts when he took me back to my life on Sellier; we weren't conversing with words, and I never knew it. I have that ability too, though partially developed, since I lived on Sellier.

Then things turned serious. Serious because, we both knew about the deeds he had done on Sellier that got him exiled, albeit for the wrong crimes. They *were bad deeds*. How could they have happened? Elvis didn't or couldn't explain that at all, but he vowed he would find out and give me what he found.

SELLIER

SELLIER'S HISTORY

C. Van Heyden

For the time being Elvis would enjoy being home; he would try to get a job or some work to support himself, and he would definitely court Regallia, or let her court him. That's more or less what happened he told me.

About this time, I started picking up that Master Chip Ty Dick wanted to go out peacefully from his mortal existence. I observed him carefully writing things into a diary of sorts, and carefully going around his acreage tending to the plants. He told me soon I would be fully in charge and we both bowed knowingly to each other. He also encouraged me to look for students and to take only the sincere ones. He had put an ad, unbeknownst to me, in the daily Fenshan weekly paper, and students began arriving to be interviewed. One such student reminded me of myself two and one half years earlier, and I agreed he would be my first pupil in the martial arts. Without a word of guidance from the Master, I began to educate my new pupil as Master Dick had educated me.

Now, returning to Elvis on Sellier. Seems Regallia discovered Elvis' facility for space engineering and his ability to dance, both of which interested her, and found him work with an allied firm that made those fast moving whatever they were flying devices he had glimpsed on first arriving. The dancing he didn't go into but I gathered the folks on Sellier dig it a lot and are usually quite good at it. I will admit, with the perspicacity of the inhabitants of Sellier I shuddered to think what they might do to Elvis when or if they found out what acts he had perpetrated there.

Apparently Regallia was not so much impressed that Elvis was a revenant as much as that he took the chance of hitching a ride with the alien space jockeys. She did not like them at all and told Elvis that he was a very lucky guy to have not been molested by them. She *was* going to have him get scanned for implants, but he sweet-talked her out of doing that, saying that he was awake the whole journey in a state of reverie much like when he would lie back in a summer hammock on a tranquil day and contemplate his future. And he messaged me thus.

I've been trying to learn from Regallia anything about *those days* when tyranny and counter tyranny swept Sellier. She told me that according to her recollection the main problem, the one that caused political discord was simply the stupidity of the governing bodies to deal with the population increase. They couldn't keep up with the demands for infrastructure without taking drastic steps to curb procreation, and this infuriated the populace, and allowed insurgents to rise who championed against those in power who advocated severe birth control and limiting family sizes. Now, that was a curse no longer because by necessity, out of the devastation from all that conflict came men, and some women who found ways and who developed technology for making inhabitable spaces habitable for people, for increasing the food supply, quite cleverly by the way, for improving the retention capability for students so they could graduate much earlier and have more to offer the work-a-day world in the bargain. Overall the atmosphere turned from solemn protective to nearly *vie libre*. Let people live. Trust them to do the right thing, without interfering. I told her in turn that I had been one who challenged the authority of leaders. She acknowledged that without comment.

Much of what I have learned from wise Regallia could be put to use by governing bodies on Earth to their mutual success. For instance, the complicated law system and the writing of enormously long bills that go on for hundreds even thousands of pages doesn't exist on Sellier. The limit on pages here is 100, and few bills ever reach that total. So lawyers don't abound here, whereas artisans are everywhere. As I said the need for law and order, much less police is undeniably superfluous; it just doesn't get that serious.

Not that crimes don't ever occur. In fact, there was one just a few days back, and pretty heinous too, seems a man, a crazed man, took a machete type weapon and proceeded to chop up another man accused of seducing his wife away from him. Found out later, the guy was a married man with family and wasn't the guy he was after in the first place. What was the penalty? The man who did the chopping inherited the dead man's wife and children to support for life on his recommendation. Seems fair to me.

I don't know when I am going to reveal my crimes of the past, but it won't be long. It can't be. Amongst very honest people its rather painful withholding misdeeds.

SELLIER

THE QUESTION

C. Van Heyden

Elvis related an observation to me one evening early that I think is worthy of inclusion. There was on Earth an "Age of Reason" but there on Sellier it is an age of Aesthetics, and that is far more sustainable since it results in tangible products that support life, instead of "ologies" which have the tendency to support conflicts. I was still worried for Elvis' safety because of the potential reaction that lies beneath the calm exterior of most beings when memories of cruel times are reactivated. Remember his counter-vigilante group acted to hasten the demise of the Almighty and civilization as they knew it at the time. Even though many of the inhabitants there were capable artisans and artists, there were also many who made their living supporting them with the mundane tasks of existence and these beings had the ability to recall the past and their past lives. So, even without a reaction they could well up as a force and destroy Elvis or put him on an interminable series of amends tasks.

So, Elvis decided he would confess all to his new love, Regallia, and see if she would understand. And as it turned out, in relating the details, he also touched upon the one murder he was truly ashamed of, Colton, and this had been Regallia's brother. But Elvis would not propitiate his death to Regallia, one, because he knew that she would take it as a weakness, and two, he was confessing and this was not the time to make right the wrongs he committed. Instead he continued to right up to and past the time of his summons, accusal, imprisonment and eventual banishment from Sellier. This ended, Regallia asked him a question he dreaded hearing..."What will you propose to balance the acts you've committed when it comes time to report them to the authorities so that you can remain here with good conscience?" And this he did not know, so he did not answer.

SELLIER

EXPIATION

C. Van Heyden

When I finally communicated his transmissions to Catherine, she quickly proposed that I help her locate Serena Amparo so she could go and join Elvis on Sellier. Then I had to explain quite at length that he had found a new love, and that even if I could locate Serena, there was no chance of repeating Elvis's success since he had had very luckily the token they desired. This was the final crushing event for her.

The day finally came also when Chip Ty Dick, Taekwondo Master and my mentor left his mortal self. In a ceremony that dated back centuries, I and my new student wrapped the Master's body in silk bandages and carried it to the far extent of his property, and there in the evening burned the remains to ashes, as was his instructions. The next day the cold ashes were added to the berm for a blue lotus plant newly added to the garden the Master tended all his life. He left me complete instructions on mentoring students, on taking care of the grounds, and some vintage books on the Ramayana and other Hindu writings covering the skill of shape-shifting. I could not tell Elvis all that had transpired for I was as yet not adept as he in long distance telepathy, and anyway Elvis had his own problems to face on Sellier and would not countenance much anymore what happened on Earth, even to a *blood brother* of sorts.

While I took care of the proper disposal of Master Dick's body, Elvis had come upon a plan after contemplating how to soften the blow of his evil deeds when he revealed them to the people of Sellier, at least the city he knew as Sellier. He was not sure even his plan would be enough to keep him from being ostracized immediately from the inhabitable regions. He was sure to reveal all the tedious and degrading times he had spent on Earth and make sure his listeners would know that his exile was no dispatch to the isle of Elba.

As he told it: "I could not simply vow to never employ counter-vigilante methods again nor vow to always be a good citizen, that was already a given if you planned to live on this planet. What I could do is employ my powers to undo, at least as much of the chaos and death that remained residually in the collective psyche of Sellier from those horrendous times. As with my regressing of selective students back at Bingham University, I would take, on a non-paying basis, several citizens who were game to undertake a spiritual revisiting of those times with an aim to expunge all of or most of the *shock* that hit them. Choosing randomly from only those citizens who by actual attestation new that their subsequent lives were tainted, even warped by the foment and sheer brutality they experienced. Never telling them or indicating that they would have to purge their souls too, to get full benefit. This is my plan, this is what I'll propose when I go before the council."

Elvis didn't know, if approved, if even he would live long enough to carry out the one-on-one *deep* counseling. But he stated to me emphatically that that was the very best contribution he could make. The Council met every six months, and that was fast approaching.

C. Van Heyden

SELLIER

MAKING ALLIES

C. Van Heyden

Elvis needed friends ahead of his confession; he needed to have that security since he planned on staying on Sellier and marrying Regallia and having children and doing what he planned, not only for citizenship but for his own conscience and integrity. With friends to support him, even if he should be denounced, he would have a better go of it certainly than with only Regallia by his side. So, Elvis made every effort to create positive feelings about himself. The first way was to repeat his successes with the students at Bingham University but on Sellier.

At work, he found a co-worker who reminded him very much of Lexington back on Earth: suave, caring, well-educated but not the least snobbish. Elvis tells it this way: "Alex worked near me in propulsion and I worked in...well design and mechanical drafting but not a novice position anymore. We are about the same height and weight and we lunch together, even though he has never known me on Sellier before. We seem to just like paling around, you know like when you're kids and there's no status thing going on like later in life. He tells me all about the sub-orbital rocket ships that go everywhere and I tell him about the new *secret designs* he's not to know about until released. I said earlier the air is noticeably fresher than that on Earth, and the reason is I found, there's slightly more oxygen and nitrogen and less hydrogen in it. The rocket fuel, classified data, burns more steadily and longer because of the higher nitrogen content. For the interstellar craft only nuclear reactor fuel is used. You know what that means? I could conceivably return to Earth someday. On the other hand I could be deported again."

"I recently asked Alex if I were to be accused or even found guilty of a crime, albeit from *very* long ago, would he disown me? Alex thought about it for a moment and said, 'I wouldn't disown you, because I know you, but I would, could only give testimony as to the good traits you've shown me.' And when he had said that he asked the nature of the crime. This made me extremely uncomfortable because I didn't know whether he had been alive during that period, and I also didn't know whether I may have injured someone close to him or himself. He had never heard of The Almighty, and no recall on any planet-wide revolution. I wasn't in the clear even then because when I told him the nature of the crime he wanted details."

SELLIER

BEFORE THE HIGH COUNCIL

C. Van Heyden

That night, as Elvis tells it, something about Alex's inquiry set things on end, and he once again had a terrible dream. "I was swimming in mucous, the world was full of mucous, Everywhere I looked trees, flowers, plants, mountains, valleys were covered with mucous. Animals too. I flew high as a falcon and I could see the deserts of Sellier dripping with mucous, the plains and even uninhabitable areas stuck in that yellowish viscous and slimy substance. Even the rocket planes and suborbital conveyances: all covered in mucous. The houses and homes the parks and festival areas deluged. The enormous lakes were covered with a bubbly, frothy mucous like the turbulent backwash of a filthy canal. Nowhere could I see a location that was not inundated. Even at the poles of Sellier, there it was. I looked with horror to the double sun and it was encased in a brownish mucous."

"When I finally awoke, I was sick. Very sick. I crawled out of bed and heaved a great wad of mucous into the disposal. I can not wait another day. I'm going to the council chambers and ask for a non-scheduled hearing. If I am lucky they won't make me wait. I must relieve myself of these pressures."

With Regallia's influence, Elvis got a special audience with the council.

C. Van Heyden

...

The council chambers were somber and somewhat cold. There were six council members seated in a semi-circle facing Elvis. As he related, it was as ominous looking a council as he could have imagined. Before a gallery of interested parties he began.

"Gentlemen and gentlewomen, I have come before you with this matter of urgency, utmost to myself, in great hopes that by confessing my misdeeds *and* by proposing a project to the council to set these matters to rest, I will relieve my troubled soul of their burden while achieving thereby the consent and goodwill of the council and all citizens of Sellier, that being the chief objective of the purging."

"Given the nod to proceed by the head council member, I began the tale of The Almighty, his demise and my crimes attendant to that period. I left out nothing. I did not try to vindicate my actions in anyway, nor bring the subject of my exile and its painful details up except as sequential acts to all that came before. This time I was able to name each of the victims dispatched by the counter-vigilantes and myself, so that any citizen that was affected by or made uncertain as to why or how their comrades, spouses, brothers came to an ignominious end would be satisfied. When I was done, there was commotion in the gallery. First, I perceived the thought, 'Banish him to the uninhabitable areas'. Another thought arose, 'What will you do to atone for your crimes?' And another from the dais, 'He should not be allowed citizenship nor the right to procreate.'"

"Regallia stepped forward and asked to be heard. This granted, she eloquently began a defense for me against harsh punishment including the fact that as citizens we know how turbulent that time was in Sellier's history, and that there are few amongst us who did not commit crimes at that time worthy of censure if not severe punishment. However there were several in the gallery whose relatives were the targets of the murders, and they wanted reparations equal to the deeds. This the chairman heard and requested of me a direct response. I set out for all to perceive that I was contrite, that I was willing to attempt almost anything to achieve equality with them again short of debasing or degrading tasks, and that is when I launched the plan to alleviate the residual pain, that as citizens of Sellier knew, was inherent to life and to living through embattled times."

"As I proceeded to relate my success on Earth with the technique first used with you, the gallery became noticeably less agitated. After finishing the details of how I would go about administering such contribution there was only one adversary. The one who wanted to deny procreation and marriage rights as well, even if I were successful. This then was a stalemate until Alex, unbeknownst to me in the gallery came forward with words of conciliatory effect. His argument as simple: He declared his knowledge of my worth, that I was capable of honest work and production, that I was trustworthy, and that I could have chosen to not reveal the crimes and simply lived amongst us *in cognito.*"

I doubt that the enmity in the one council member was assuaged; nonetheless the council voted that my project be admitted for consideration but based on close scrutiny and testimony by the participants. But, if successful by report thereby, that the amends project be incorporated into my full existing lifetime and if possible taught to others who would or could use it for reconciling their transgressions with society. I was thanked for my confessions, as are all citizens who come forth for absolution, and in this I already felt more like one of the true inhabitants of Sellier than when I lived here before.

SELLIER

SENTENCED

C. Van Heyden

It made complete sense, after the hearing, that Elvis should deliver his *magical* beneficence to as many individuals as physically possible. He could of course also, after much success appeal the life term sentence to do this service, and the wise council would I'm sure agree. Either way he was conditionally accepted as a valid citizen again on his home planet, that being the entire objective of his confessions.

There was, according to Elvis's report, some scurrilous warnings posted anonymously around the city to scare inhabitants from accepting this *dubious service* as the posted handbills stated. But within a few weeks, the powerful effects of his abilities were overwhelmingly echoed by its beneficiaries, and the handbills disappeared for good. It was about this time, or maybe a few months later that I got a sudden transmission from Elvis and the nature of it made me shiver.

Those aliens that had dropped Elvis off many months earlier had come back. And they wanted something, Elvis didn't want to give them. They wanted the location of the teleportation station on Earth. Elvis relates: apparently, this was only one of many visits to Sellier which is why they recognized how to get here from the map created by Lexington. I perceived that they wanted to either capture, destroy or subjugate that outpost. I still could not communicate directly with them, but Regallia could which is why she despised them so much. As the discussion grew heated between myself, Regallia and the chief alien it appeared that they only wanted the technology at the station. From Regallia I got that this was a cover. Having no idea as to how the *other aliens* at the station would react, such as an all out war I chose not to divulge its location. Then a most curious dialog emerged. The chief alien turned the conversation over to another alien which I presume was like to us a librarian. That alien began a very in depth and from what Regallia translated a very earnest plea for the information. The "librarian" stated time and place and form and event on every Earth war, major conflict, and civil commotion going back hundreds of years. Every assassination of a monarch or president and any country's leaders as well. The alien stated emphatically that the outpost station was in almost every case the feeder tube for instigators of these times of upheaval. In exchange for the location they would do their best to eliminate the outpost.

That was enough for me to act. My education at Bingham had taught me that wars were constantly being created to further one party's agenda or another, and most were started by religions for the main purpose to control populaces. I gave them what they wanted. Joshua, I want you to monitor the major military actions on planet Earth so that one day when you can reply to my transmissions you'll be able to corroborate or not what the librarian stated was fact. If the aliens are successful there should be a noticeable reduction.

C. Van Heyden

SELLIER

ENVOI

C. Van Heyden

I n the second full year of Elvis' return to Sellier and cohabitation with Regallia, Elvis petitioned for reduction of sentence imposed and got a mitigated sentence, based on sufficient reports from citizens that he had helped to remove the stigma of those days when Sellier had gone to the dogs. His life was no longer pinioned to an interminable assignment. Justice had been served.

For myself, I did finally acquire the ability to telepathically communicate with Elvis, which is why those who have read these confessions can with complete confidence believe them and his story. And one more thing, and perhaps you may have also become aware of it, the outpost was destroyed. There have been fewer major conflicts since that occurrence.

C. Van Heyden

Does it take a Samson or Hercules to
overthrow one's barriers and obstacles?

In ON CONQUERING THINGS the author both
humorously and not humorously tells of his
subduings in life with stories of how conquering
things *in life* is the main duty of a person,
regardless of the odds.

"Here is a rare and interesting glimpse into the
fertile mind of a budding storyteller."

— Richard A. McCullough, The Rich Writers Coach™

C. Van Heyden

SELLIER

All letters addressed to the author will be given immediate care
and response. They can be addressed to:

Velvet Gloves Publishing

1208 Brooks Mill Circle

Hermitage, TN 37076

Include an SASE